The Door of My Heart

Maxine Tynes

Pottersfield Press
Lawrencetown Beach, Nova Scotia
1993

To R. G. Fredericks, mentor and beloved friend.

Rod and Brenda — both of you counted as cherished links in my wondrous chain of life.

Printed in Canada

Copyright Maxine Tynes 1993

All rights reserved. No part of this publication may be reproduced or transmitted in any form or by any means, electronic or mechanical, including photocopying, or by any information storage or retrieval system, without permission in writing from the publisher.

Canadian Cataloguing in Publication Data

Tynes, Maxine.

    The door of my heart
    ISBN 0-919001-81-5

    I. Title.

PS8589.Y54D66   1993   C811'.54   C93-098605-9
PR9199.3.T96D66 1993

Cover photograph by Lesley Choyce

This book was produced with the financial assistance of Multiculturalism Canada — The Secretary of State for Multiculturalism and Citizenship.

Pottersfield Press greatfully acknowledges the ongoing support of the Nova Scotia Department of Tourism and Culture as well as the Canada Council.

Pottersfield Press
Lawrencetown Beach
R.R. 2, Porters Lake
Nova Scotia B0J 2S0

Contents

The Poet as Whole-Body-Camera   5

Cat on a Clothesline
Cat on a Clothesline   9
Let's Just Be Dark   10
Desmond Morris Explained the Kiss   11
Time   12
Raising the Heart of Women   13
The Door of My Heart   14
Those Men Who Prey on Women   16
Lu-Lu-Lulu   19
Cat Eyes at the Window   20
The Politics of Knees and Skirting   21

Rolling Thunder Titans
The Woman I am in my Dreams   25
Iron Love   27
Sugarcane   28
Gait Gait Gait Gait   30
Looking, Always Looking   31
Post Polio   32
Fear of Falling   33
Roll Me Up; Roll Me Down/ Mobile-Mobility   34
Handprints on the Wall   35
Winter Alone   36

Cat's Eye on the World
Exotic Bird   39
Graffiti Portrait   40
What's Wrong With This Picture   41

Lattice Alone	43
Dancing the Rim of the Glass Ceiling	44
Having Faith in Some Woman Named Ella	46
No Laughing Matter	47
And Again	48
Prelude to the Rock	50
This Dartmouth at Alderney Gate, 1990	52
The Portable Muse	54
First Poem	56
Let There Be Sex...	57
We Demand the Right to Pee	61
In this Country	66

Stories

Talk That Talk	71
Open Windows	77

Through My Classroom Door

Ici on Parle Egalite	83
How Many Children Do You Have, Miss	84
Grad Portrait Gallery	85
High School Confidential	86
Head Count: Black Students...	87
Too Few of You	88
Class Change: Young Lions on the Tide	90

Black Star Rising

Black Star Rising	93
Zora in My Heart	94
The Dream of Dogs and Presidents	95

The Poet As Whole-Body Camera

These are the poems that punctuate my life. They are the lens, the shutter, the eye of this whole-body camera that I am. I see. I feel. I travel the path both broad and narrow. I snap up shots/thoughts/images of everywhere. I take the measure of all pain and pleasure, of your life and mine.

I roll like/as/for/ with those legions of Rolling Thunder Titans demanding place and accessibility agenda. I raise the flag on the personhood and on the imperative of feminist, womanist, abled/dis/abled body politic heart and soul. And I pluck at the heart-strings of Eros enroute to love.

This, then, is the realm of the poet-woman. Under canopy of West Coast mountains; along the craggy shores of the Avalon in Newfoundland. It is always the same.

This long and cherished pursuit of the Muse. She calls and she beckons. I reach and I follow to the edge and to the precipice of what is and what will be my song in words. My word-song of poetry.

And if you seek my journey. And if our isms fit and mesh and meld us heart to heart to heart. Then, through this journey of poet and of those who read, those who follow, we shall go two by two by many, many fold.

To seek, to test and to test the thrust, the parry of thought and word and ism and image. Together.

CAT ON A CLOTHESLINE

Cat On A Clothesline

If I were a cat on a clothesline
I would do a
delicate cat's paw balance
between your back pockets
a cat's hair would separate me
from your most secret of secrets
me
that cat on a clothesline
you
the hollow wind-body
filling each sleeve
bellied out in the paunch of every shirt

the cat on a clothesline
calculates her every move
cannot bridge the distance
from clothesline to heartbeat
is gathered
grey and black and taut
is launched in cat-flight
is gone

Let's Just Be Dark

Let's just be dark, then
being shade and shadows that walk upright
being night in daytime

Let's just be dark, then
the dark side of things
sifting light through pigment darkly
illuminating some deep soul from within

Let's just be dark, then
with arms and legs hued in dark oak,
ash, mahogany
this body bronzed or blackened like trees

Let's just be dark, then
eyes and teeth flicker neon
against this sun darkly
clothes and colours hang like banners

Let's just be dark, then
neither friend nor foe of sunlight
casting nightshade from the to and fro
of this dark sojourn through the life.

Desmond Morris Explained The Kiss

Desmond Morris explained the kiss
on *Larry King Live*
and made me smile
to hear him intellectualize
'all that tonguing' he said
connecting us far, far back in time
to some cave-dwelling mother
masticating brontosaurus loins and mouth-feeding them
to her Cro-magnon babe-in-arms

Desmond Morris
let me tell you the kiss
let me fast-forward you to the now of passion
cushioned on lips poised and
moistened for the contact of Eros
lips swollen to the shape and lure of Venus
lips that speak the ebb and flow of love
lips
lips
the pucker and sound of the word
mirrors and anticipates
the deep and luscious doing of the kiss
I am and I do that kiss
I receive and I give that kiss
that invites and drowns in the sea of passion.

Time

I savour time like some toothsome filet;
some breast of chicken ticking of the clock
peeling back the skin of seconds
                            seconds
                            seconds;
seasoning minutes: 5, 10, 15, 20 at a time;
sauteing hours, by the half
quarter, and 60-minute whole;
Time, done to a turn;
Time, turned out on the warmed up,
warmed-over platter of my life;
Time, garnished with:
- to be early
- to be late
- not enough time for;
Time freeze-dried, pre-packaged,
simulated into a reasonable facsimile
of your watch, clock radio, digital time-piece;
Big Ben on your kitchen wall.
Time;
From time-to-time;
Time after time;
Timely;
Timetable; timing;
Out of time;
It is time.

Raising The Heart Of Women
For those women who are coming forward to stand centre stage in this country and who are reflecting us women back at twice our size!

To raise the heart of women
in that room
to raise the heart of women
in the fray
that is womanist and feminist
and humanist and full of accessibility, yours and mine
and a world view that is inclusionary
that is backyard, pay-cheque, budget-cut, wage-freeze,
unemployment, welfare line familiar;

That speaks in a language that is
unemployed, homeless, disabled, denied access, underpaid,
that is fighting for voice and place
that speaks in a language that is woman and Black
and Aboriginal
that is immigrant, that is Francophone
that is denied freedom of choice
that is working poor, that is over-taxed
that is full of this multiple agenda
and that is reaching, reaching for the light.

The Door Of My Heart

For AIDS VIGIL, 1991; Dartmouth, N.S.

Open the door of my heart
walk through
dance through
open the door of my heart
there is something there
waiting for you
an easy chair, beside me to sit
a cup of cheer
a smile
a letter waiting
a pot of tea
a hand to hold
a hug to enfold you and me.

Open the door of my heart
let's both walk through
let's find a street
a bench a job a school
a friend a co-worker
someone, someplace who is
looking at us with eyes that see
with a mind and compassion
like that door of my heart
so big and big and open for you.

Here's the door of my heart
it's a street
it's a house with a garden
and a number on the door
it's a mother, child, partner, father, friend,
co-worker, sister, brother, lover
who knows the joy of staying close;

It's a mind just turned around
from narrow to open and informed
and broad and empowered
to care and to feel and to love
and to be there
just, just to be there;

It's a warm and cozy corner
it's that photo, that smile
and that memory
and the making of that memory
all of those memories.

That door of my heart
that open door;
it's the start and the finish of every embrace
it's the smile and the tear in somebody's eye
it's the dance and the fire of all the stars,
and all the suns,
and all the flags of every end
and of all beginnings.

That door of my heart
walk through
dance through.

Those Men Who Prey On Women

Those men who prey on women
who sharpen their teeth, their tongue
on the lives of women
who grow big on a diet of
power and control

those men who stalk,
who follow
who mark their prey by gender
and by the tissue of flesh
and of purse strings

Where did you develop a taste for pain?
What cutlery do you wield so deftly?
What palate cries out for the angst
that is the pain
 the terror
 the victim that you make
of a woman's heart
her soul
her flesh
her skin
her life?

you, who are the men who wield power and pain
at the end of your fist
 your word
 your deadly intention
 your penis

I
We see you in the mirror of life
your reflection is small
and, smaller still
while I,

we women walk upright in this place
flashing our anger and our tears
like breastplates

We watch, ox-eyed
at this feast of man-fist
man-word
of deadly male intention
and of the man-like effigy of you
in your pants
petulant and small
like an errant child
wanting to be big and out
before its time

all of this you bring to the feast
that you make of the prey
that you mark by gender

I
we
the earth recoils at your foot-fall

I
we witness your trade in terror
and in pain of those who are women
we witness the currency of
fear and of flesh

we see you taste the bones and
the life of Anita, of Jane,
of the maids of Montreal
and of her
and of her

Who next to impale upon your fork
   your blade

your fist
your word
your deadly male intention
your penis?

THOSE MEN WHO STALK
WHO FOLLOW
who prey upon women
we serve you notice
The kitchen is closed.
We are not on your menu.

Lu-Lu-Lulu

When I stand beside you
in and under that fiery, glinting
bush and umbra of your hair
you don't know how you electrify me
how you spark and light me everywhere.
That throaty ha-ha laugh
both masks and heralds
the neutron dance of music and magic
from the Lulu soul and brain of you.
This short, short black and blacker woman
sees and feels and taps a sisterhood
a sister-vision that we have
that we spiralled together to and from
You, from some Celtic Antigonish spark and magic
Me, from the African Canadian heartbeat
of my displaced Diaspora life.
You and I
we hear the same ancient whisper
that called us together long ago
that flung us into each other's eye and embrace
on street corners
and in galleries, over and over again
hearing and seeing and wanting each other's work forever.
Lulu,
when I stand with you
in our black and fiery aura
I catch fire
You catch dark.

Cat Eyes At The Window

Snow falls
making a mid-winter panorama
of the restaurant window
and,
I think of you watching these same
wet-fat-lazy-lacy flakes fall
somewhere,
on some street
away from me.
A girl walks by,
leaning, muffled, into the snow-wind.
I think of you.
Clatter of forks.
The chatter of strangers.
Neil Young instead of muzak
on the restaurant airwaves;
snowflakes swirl and dance,
and grow fat and fall, together.
Like a cat at this window I see
that world outside
this world
this room
these thoughts.

The Politics of Knees and Skirting

Skirting
Skirting
band around the waist
small
two hands' span
or, more girth
eased and eased by forgiving elastic
smoothing of fabric
over hip
flank
trunk
belly
hugged and silhouetted to compliant curves
or full and luscious drift and billow of fabric
cotton silk wool rayon
to drape
and to camouflage
generous flesh
big legs at ease under benevolent drape
and pleating
skirting the issue
of dimpled knees and thunderous thighs.

And now
some sylph-like ingenue
slipping by
her enigmatic micro-mini
a flag and a traffic light
her legs
powerful and charged with the light of androgyny
carry her on and on
past my stares and silent, silent cheering and wondering
just when she too will feel her legs — all up and down
will read new dimensions in her mirror
will call for elastic

more; then more
will sigh with contentment as the fabric falls and falls lower and lower still.
When knees become a mystery.

ROLLING THUNDER TITANS

The Woman I Am In My Dreams

The woman I am in my dreams
is taller than I am
and sees the world as she walks
unlike me with eyes on every step
   with eyes ever and always on the ground
that woman walks only when
she feels like not running
not jogging
the woman I am in my dreams
lifts one leg effortlessly over the other
crosses them
high up on the knee
   the hip
   the thigh
not just at the ankle like I do.

The woman I am in my dreams
breaks all the rules about shoes
wears them high and red
with killer spike heels
   moves from Nikes to spikes
   and the kind of pumps
   that go with a dress
   and having your hair done

the woman I am in my dreams
her legs are straight and sure
they don't fly out from under her
they don't hide under long skirts
her legs and feet are well
they speak for her in footsteps on the road
they laugh at hills and
at rolling, unforgiving gravel

they dialogue with ice and snow
and they always win that argument

the woman I am in my dreams
I wake up and carry part of her
with me everywhere.

Iron Love

Mid-coitus
reaching up
I climb the railed headboard of my
century-old brass and iron bed
to roll close and closer
to my able-bodied lover.
I think of a rating scale
of kudos for a lover who will
pick up, lift, shift lifeless legs and feet
some nerve-dead body-part whatever
with blase grace and sweet and tender care:
10 stars or kisses for shifting my leg
8 for positioning my foot just right
15 stars or kisses for remembering
to never-never touch my toes.

I climb that railed headboard
reaching over and through the plush army of bears
teddies on patrol.
I climb that railed headboard
rolling close and closer to you each time.
You smile and cuddle.
I climb that railed headboard,
I smile and even laugh
during that hand-over-hand necessity.
You, my able-bodied lover,
You think it is my original Everlast love-play,
I smile and thank my wisdom at falling in love
with this elegant old bed.
It moves me.

Sugarcane

This cane
this third leg
this thump-step-thumper
this badge-flag-symbol of
my desire to stand up
  to keep up
  to walk up
  to step up
to always be up, not down
  not flat on my back
  like an up-ended turtle,
  flailing for dignity.

This cane.
I love it like a lover.
I caress it up and down,
I finger its nicks and its contours,
I smell and behold it
knowing its heft, its length.

This constant constant constant
having beauty and consistency
turned on a lathe
looking like natty bamboo
getting stares and touches
and questions from admiring friends and strangers.

This constant cane companion.
I both love and possess you
am confident with you in hand
bewildered when you fall from my sight.

You fall on the floor,
others rush to pick you up.
I say to leave you lying there at my feet

like a faithful and ready golden Lab.

And if you should break
or if I should lose you
my fear, my fear of falling
without you leaps up in my heart, becoming real.

I look and there you are
lying at my feet, my golden Lab.
My cane.

Gait Gait Gait Gait Gait

I bang one foot down on the ground
I drag the other behind me
I bang one foot down on the ground
I drag the other behind me
My footprints look like
a one-legged dinosaurus
A draggin' footed woman
just foot-thump-draggin' along.

Looking, Always Looking

Woman in the mall
on the corner
waiting for your bus
I resent your stares
those eyes that you impale me with
those eyes hot, pierced and grafted
to my leg that drags
my foot that flaps and hesitates
my signature limp and gait.
Be like the child at your side.
Be honest and ask, or
just see me like a fence or a tree
or like anybody passing by
instead of giving me
those hot and unforgiving stares
reserved for the deformed
the halt and the lame
and the mistakes left behind by dogs.

Post Polio

post polio
send polio
post it up, up, and away from
this body
these bodies
my body
post polio syndrome
charted and documented
by the victim participants
those ones told in the '50s.

"Don't take a dip in the public swimmin' hole."
post it away
this droning, droning syndrome
relentless anchor albatross
leg ankle hip back neck arm bone
albatross souvenir of 1955.

Fear of Falling: Releasing Thanks To Two Hearty Pairs

I fell once
on those brick revival unforgiving waterfront streets.
Actually, the fall from grace was twice;
the poet woman orator wordsmith
down
down
and down
feeling the bite of brick and stone
elevated to my feet
by two male and fleeting strangers
small heroic men
undaunted by the task of raising
this large and heavy woman-body.
Twice this happened one summer.
Different times
Different Halifax corners
two different pairs of passing street samaritans
male levers in concert
raised my helpless bulk
dusted off my yellow dress
retrieved my errant cane
checked knees for bloody skinnings
set me on course to the ferry
then,
both times,
the pair that saved me:
four arms; four hands; four feet and legs braced and straining
The pair that saved me disappeared.

Roll Me Up; Roll Me Down/Mobile-Mobility

When I envy your wheels
When I'm stuck on hold
When streets are slick and frozen solid
When my path from here to there is an Olympic ice-sheet
When these post-polio feet and legs
cry out in protest of another step
   another step
When I need/don't want to plead my case for accessibility
in able-bodied heads.
For one crazy moment
that plays and plays back
like an endless tape-loop
I envy your chair
that speaks those sharp and mute and rolling volumes.

Handprints On The Wall

At this great and growing age
and with no children
ever in this life
of a solitary woman's home
I have handprints on the wall
high up
breast, chest, hip
belly, arm and shoulder high

I rove my thirteenth floor halls
the walls are a testimony to my passing
I reel and I totter and
I seldom fall
instead, clutching doorjambs
and windowsills
the walls chart and record my passing
my fingerprints in the colours
of lipstick and of eyeshadow

my walls blush at my passing
and never want for human touch
this woman
flying in from a night of challenge
and commitment
I fall into my walls
they keep and they hold me
and mark, hand over hand
my passage.

Winter Alone

winter solitude
memories from
my fifth
my tenth year of winter alone
behind glass
the pane of my isolation
a vast distance marked
by snow
by ice
by legs and feet undone
not heeding the neuron call
to move
to move
to jump the ice
to careen belly-to-sled
down some endless slope
a world beyond the pane
the landscape of
small friends and siblings
oblivious
in riotous hillside reverie.

THE CAT'S EYE ON THE WORLD

Exotic Bird

I really love it
when you call me
your exotic bird
your being the operative word
here, when we are so new together
and, *exotic bird*

being wonderful
you
being mindful and joyful in my colours
clothes
big shoulders
the wing-span and plumage
of the now-woman that I am.

I have been many things
to men and to friends and lovers
an endless smile
warm and comfortable arms
or someone's dark and starry, starry night
but you see my plumage
and the prow of my hips
and my leaning
a-port, astern on cane-in-hand
my rudder in a sea of
rocks and curbs and pitfalls
and you outside my door
waiting
to call me
your exotic bird.

Graffiti Portrait

the sons of Africa in the world
the young lions
rendered day-glo and impotent
against an early morning wall in corridor
he shouts an echo of practiced male plumage
in full voice
arrests and assails the poet-woman
who each day, after dawn
must skirt their gauntlet
they hail her with their epithets
of scorn
and of undisguised male invective
their vowels and consonants rain down
fall like knives
penetrate like shrapnel

her footprints
a hieroglyph of purple wound and query.

What's Wrong With This Picture?

After thirty-five plus years of
watching television
 t.v.
 the tube
 the box
I still can't see myself
I look hard and often
and everywhere
on every blue and flickering screen

I stay up round the clock
aiming and clicking the remote
in cycles of networks and channels
tracking the elusive Black face on screen
coming up empty
and snowblind in the night

the little white kids from the playground
are the big white kids
who mouth and smile out
my global news
who map and chart my weather
who sell adult diapers
and pizza and condoms and beer

don't look for the tokens in this poem
I know how to count them too well
as one talk show matriarch to the world
as one
or two
or six recycled stand-up comics
as a few all-purpose singers,
rappers, celluloid cops-and-robbers
and well-meaning but never caught in a kiss or a clinch
neighbour/assistant/partner/friend/pal/cohort/sidekick

the little white kids are
minding the t.v. store
my local evening news
never comes to me in Blackface

don't look to the airwaves for salvation
early morning radio
is a snowstorm of Celtic inflection
or of Middle America
no raucous or ethnic dialect
to wake up to
or to hum along to in traffic
unless its a soundtrack of
Michael or Luther or Aretha or Diana

only Cable opens a door, a mike
a stage
and then, for the Black or minority market

the Black host and panel on Cable
talks racism and racism and racism

you'll find no respite from the snowstorm here

and when I aim the clicker that turns you off
when my t.v. screen is still and black
you glow; etched and neon
eyes and lips waiting to
whiten and fill my world again.

Lattice Alone

You know that lattice
white and picture perfect
sometimes green
in up-market gardens and
making deck walls in the 'burbs
it holds a secret
it conceals and it homogenizes
it muffles the deep and aching thud
of slaps
of fists
of bereft tears in the night.

Dancing The Rim Of The Glass Ceiling

Those dinosaurs who walk among us
slapping their tails on the ground
dragging us into
the craters of their footprints
they leave droppings the size of abandoned bombs

we fall
and we fall into the crater of
the dinosaur
agenda books fall to the ground
fall open to the pages
which track bank balances
and the mapping of cycles
both economic and menstrual

we cling and scramble
at the lip of the crater
hands black and white
and poor and young and feminist and disabled
claw at the rim
exchange palm-prints
with each other

our breasts, your sexual preference
somebody's ideology
these are our stepladders
we snag on broken rungs and false promises

I reach up
you grab the rim
the dinosaur slaps his tail on the ground
I/we lose our balance
and as we fall again
                again
the dinosaur parades by

dressed for Bay Street
and for the battleground
he opens his mouth to laugh
                        to eat

we belly up to the rim
we hear the dinosaur
belch out our name.

Having Faith In Some Woman Named Ella

Having faith in some woman named Ella
a small silhouette in the spotlight
her scat
her vibrato always true
always drowns out the computer

some small singer-woman named Ella
clinging small and delicate in a
dangle from some mike-stand

a splash of skin smooth and black and blue
1940s processed hair
singing the blues to avid bigots of the 40s, the 50s
and like Dinah, like Billie
like Oscar and like Nat, the King of Cole
hoping for a home-folks billet in the BlackBelt
dreaming for days of the dining room
and crisp linen
French service

in the spotlight
the glitter of sequins plays your face neon
checkerboards the face of Ella to the world.

No Laughing Matter

*In homage to Carrie Mae Weems and for the installation NO LAUGH-
ING MATTER: Dalhousie Art Gallery, March 1992.*

We stand in galleries
swallowing cubism and
landscapes whole

but at No Laughing Matter
we clutch our hearts
and our imperatives
and we laugh that
15 year-old-in-the-funeral-parlour laugh
while Carrie Mae Weems
and Guerilla Girls
laugh
and laugh
and weep from the walls.

And Again

And again
so like the long ago of our first
our first
rolling into the vault
and ocean of the other
so like the pull of that long ago first
our first
treading the shoals and the shallows of
first touch
first touch and kiss and kiss
so like the ebb and riptide of that
long ago first
our first
the dual eye of breast
of arm
of hip
of leg, flank, cheek, belly
the test and exploration of palm
on palm
in and out of dark and liquid hollow
the slow dance to the brink of Eros
the fox-fire waltz upon its rim
the free fall fall and
whirl to vortex
down and down
devoured and devouring
every sense of *of* and *to*
and with
and with
being one
then not
then one and one
speaking in the orbit of
skintalk
skintalk from some

immeasurable sometime
the call from who my womanself was
before the count of time
speaking in the tongue of Eros
and of Venus

You/I/we light and quench
those fires that ignite
and burn from ice to ember
always, embers waiting.

Prelude To The Rock

On the discovery of my love of Newfoundland—National Book Week 1993 on the Avalon Peninsula. (For Barbara and John, delight of our heart at Galecliff.)

...the coastline
the music
the food
the lore

no preparation for the treasure
and for the wonder of
this island place
this Newfoundland
this rough-hewn jewel
on our most eastern Atlantic coast
with her sharp and rocky shores
and shoals
breasting the sea

no hot and breathy whispers shared
of the pleasure of this place
the layer on layer of true-hearted spirit
against the odds of history
of politics come and gone
and of the gods of the fates
...the hungry sea and rocks
sated and unsated by the lives of Newfoundland
gone to untimely rest beneath the waves

I come to you, Newfoundland,
a novice from the mainland
from up along
from away
half-steeped in some gauzy thought of who you are
the best way to come to the Avalon
through the fog

to the heart and
to the soul of you

I bring my talk of crime and fear
in the urban wasteland of mainland life
you simply say, as wide-eyed I learn,
that this is a place of no locks and of open doors
I say it's a place of open hearts
of people who see others and know
and sing and story and say
just who they are

these cliffs and coves of the Avalon
from New Harbour to Upper Island Cove
my eyes
my heart
my sense of place
of truth
of home and away
newly known and knit together
enroute from Spaniard's Bay
to Carbonear
to Bay Roberts
and back to the heart of hearts of
Upper Island Cove
hold a place for me
hold a place for me
don't want to be known as
that one from the mainland
that one from away

I want to be the one from up along
that one from the Bay

The Coda...
discovery of connection to
folk waiting to belong to me.

This Dartmouth At Alderney Gate, 1990
To commemorate the new Dartmouth Library, Alderney Gate, and the naming of The Maxine Tynes Room on this date June 14, 1990.

What proud destiny lay before us
As the Alderney came into the waters
and to the land of this place
This Dartmouth
Sister city to Halifax
Jewel in the crown of the Basin and of the Harbour

Spilling forth forebears,
early people
the folk who became one with
the land
the green hills, and with
the giving and yielding Aboriginal people here.

And what about my folk
the displaced Africans?
How did they come here?
Some surely as free persons.
Some surely as not.
All to be
and to become
and to build Dartmouth
with and for and alongside
the Alderney
the MicMac
the Loyalists
and those who came after.

We stand here
at the wonder of this new
Alderney Gate
Drive
Alderney library

With 1990 eyes
we see and we stand
and we are this new Dartmouth
in the shadow and in the sun of
Commercial Street
The Dartmouth Park
Silver's Hill
all the mayors, past and present
the Rope-Works
the Star Skate-Works
the steel-and-iron Shipyard
of my father's daily bread
the train
    train
    train
salute of ferries knitting the
harbour waves
the One North Street home of
my little Black girlhood
gone, but not forgotten
where Joe and Ada raised us
to salute Dartmouth
and ourselves with the same heart.
Now,
standing in the shadow
and in the sun of this Dartmouth
here and now
embracing all of Dartmouth
here and gone
and here again in our hearts.

The Portable Muse

Never begin to write a poem at the mall
you will not get to end it there
the to-ing
the fro-ing of the artificial populace
the mob of shopping
the looking and the talking
and the tsk-tsk-tsking
over prices and over taxes
taxes which stack up
like cordwood behind overblown pricetags
taxes which lay in wait
for shoppers lured by the
pseudo-pitch of sales and hype

wary and unwary
we are the consumers
lock-step
enchanted and entranced by
the mind seduction Muzak
thrumming; always there
that almost-tune that drugs us
and drags us along
like gaily dressed automatons
to the check-out
we dig deep
we flick crisp bills
fresh from the cash machine enroute
the loonies clatter
drop and roll from hand
to hand to till

I sit before and after
with this poem in progress
my gaze aligned with the
escalator in the middle-distance

the up and down play and change
of in-house shoppers
they rise and fall as easily as do the prices

the sharp and fuzzy paging voice
announces something akin to names
and license plate numbers
the Muzak does its work
my mind plays in a loop
my lazy eye can drift from
corner to corner
from windows of leather
of cotton
of books
of cholesterol free edible everything
the allure of FOR SALE in every
primary/neon hue and dimension
the scalloped edge of a woman shopper's
fuschia sweater against white cotton
catches my eye and holds it
a kid goes by stuffing in ice-cream
a couple walks by
enmeshed in the feel of each other
adults drift by
dressed pyjama-like in neon and denim
like children
a couple talk and gesture in anger
she stalks away
he turns to his coffee
all the babies cry in all the languages of the world

Does The Muse visit the mall?
do aesthetics dally there?
am I really writing this poem at the mall?
will it truly find an end and a completion?
I think of new purple socks in my bag
I'll wear them when I bring this poem to you tonight.

First Poem

this should have been
the first poem of you
sharing the smoke and the shadow that you are
telling all
and telling nothing

ten hours
of the poet, back and forth
skirting the net of
sound and reason and fury and logic
with you

it is only after then
after ten hours of you
and
with you in and out of
calm and anger and the fatigue of silliness

after my words and yours
circling
and dropping like the plummet of a mousing hawk-in-flight
only then
do I know this first poem of you.

Let There Be Sex
Let There Be Love
Let There Be Power
Let There Be Lies

And so to the shouting stage
come these two who are all of us
to parade and to inventory
their past and their present selves
to be all and nothing at all
to themselves
to each the other
to reveal and to dissemble
and to construct and reconstruct
the tract and the tissue of
tears and the truth

and so we are the chorus of
this everyman
this everywoman

we/they resurrect and bury
the life/the work they once shared
and dared to make bold and malleable
in the face of power and of eros

this Anita and this Clarence
this woman and this man
this Pygmalion and this Galatea
this Tristan and this Isolde
this Sampson and this Delilah
this woman and this man

when sex becomes love
when love becomes power

when power becomes a lie
when the Fourth Estate is
the tribunal and the crucible

when the past is the present
when the moment is made
when the word is made omnipotent

ten years ago
the currency and
the climate of sex
          of love
             of power
was an open market
a thrusting sea
for the ebb and flow of
women and men
astride that tide of
thrust and parry
the powerplay of climbing
of using and leading
and following
of mentor and of protegee

when the hand that rocked
the status quo
straightened a tie
felt a thigh
smoothed a skirt
shuffled a flirtatious glance or word
or whispered into the stacked deck of
stock reports, lies, stats and spreadsheets

Oh my libido as I climb
Oh my libido as I mentor
Oh my libido as I sit at your feet
Oh my libido as I loosen my tie

Oh my libido as I seek promotion
Oh my libido as I promote you
Oh my libido as I lead the way
Oh my libido as you follow
Oh my libido as the curtain rises
on the powerplay

Oh my libido as we invent/reinvent
assume roles in the powerplay

Oh my libido as I/we/you
invent and reinvent the script
this language of sex
        of love
        of power
        of the future lie

Oh my libido as first you, then I
am in turn, a Caesar for the other
and then, we each, in turn
become that unknown factor in the equation

Who is Caesar?
Who is Brutus?
Et tu, Clarence?
Et tu, Anita?

We become a willing and
hungry chorus for you
our appetite for promise
matched only by your
ready stream of lies and dated panache

from Washington to the world
we tuned in
turned dials
compared notes

held back tears
shed tears
called friends and made revelations
called friends and made amends
turned our bedrooms and
our boardrooms into
some collective shouting stage

tore the names of old lovers out
of old datebooks
held them up to the light
flushed the torn up bits away.

We Demand The Right To Pee

For my friend and activist/dramatist/rolling-thunder man of the world, David Shannon; at Independence '92 International Conference on Disability, Vancouver, B.C.

We demand the right to pee
here at this conference site
and to be free to
come and go
to and fro with dignity
       with dignity
we caucus and we lay bare
our hearts
and our commitments
in concurrent sessions
on disability this and that
like attendant care
economic access
education with full integration
and sexuality
and sexuality
then
we roll out here
or we thump, we hop
we crutch, we limp
we lead each other
we limp out here
to the middle ground
to this main street
of Independence '92
and things fall apart
things fall apart
as the visually-challenged delegates
have no braille maps
or agenda pages
till day three

till day three

they lobby for all of us
as we demand the right to pee
as we demand the right to pee

things fall apart
as this man with the head
and the heart of a lion
makes one circuit of the site
then two, then three
until he finds the hidden
but still, for him,
the imperfect place to pee

as we demand the right to pee
as we demand the right to pee

things fall apart
as I drag my protesting legs and feet
the walking miles
from the registration mania
to the far and distant and
obscure lounge for performers
up or down to some floor of mystery
across some elevated parking lot
I straggle like some scared and awe-struck kid
my legs and feet scream the walking miles
in this city of obstacles

as we demand the right to pee
as we demand the right to pee

things fall apart
as my new-found Denver poet-woman friend
so experienced and accomplished
this activist woman of heart and soul

her words
her partner
combined, a reckoning force
writing and speaking of love and
of debunking the myth of
the accessibility buzzword
that is raised like a flag
in the media scrum

where is her choice and her control?
where is ours?
when from her chair
her questions send the able-bodied
into a frenzy and a quick-step
of disappearance

as we demand the right to pee
as we demand the right to pee

the lobby/the rally of the
visually challenged delegates
is like a flag and a banner of
our realities in our real
walking and rolling and feeling our way lives

in this City of Independence
in the nation of the world
which speaks of disability
and whose currency is challenge

We are the physically challenged
the visually challenged
the learning disabled
the hearing impaired
the mentally and the emotionally challenged
the invisibly challenged

in an earlier and more
fatalistic time
we were crippled
blind
deaf and dumb
and addle-headed
simple-minded
touched
cursed
damned
burned
shunned
hidden away
hidden away
well, we
the nation of Independence
live our own fatalism
have our current invisibility

you use the terms of
the politically correct
the buzzword of accessibility
then you give me/give us this venue
that walks and operates
like some dream of the able-bodied
and like Tiny Tim
I swallowed my misgivings
and my frustrations
at first
as these feet and legs
screamed the miles of this
temporary city and nation
of Independence
quelling my misgivings
smiling them away
so thankful to be here
to form our visible and

activist disabled nation
by this west coast mountainous sea

but we are not Tiny Tim
we are not here to suck our collective paw
for some public and political
photo opportunity
we will not say, "Please, Sir.
May I have some more?"
for we are the reality of Independence '92
we are blind with no braille to chart this site

and we demand the right to pee
and we demand the right to pee

In This Country

I'm an artist in this country
let me dance
or sing my song
of love and life
of prairie nights
of East Coast dreams
of Great Lakes waterways
I'm an artist in this country
hear my voice
let my heart sing
I'm a worker in this country
let me earn my daily bread
let me use my skill with dignity
to pave your roads
to teach your kids
to manage your banks
to deliver your milk, your mail
and your babies, too
I'm a worker in this country
I have work—with dignity—to do

But you, federal minister
you make these cuts
you don't consult
you go too far
And the P.M. who wants to be
some U.S. star
puts us on the Free Trade table
to please some global whim
in response to our cries
he says: "sink or swim"

I'm a kid in this country
don't know what I want to be
an artist or an engineer

or a teacher, maybe
but will I have a choice by then
when I'm five foot eight or six foot three?

You better stop those cuts
leave me some choice
don't leave me flat
it's only fair
let me have choice
to do and to be
what and who I want to be

I am poor in this country
and I'm a woman who's been hurt
I am homeless
I need shelter
and my hunger's getting worse
but with cuts to women's programs
my future's looking dim
I am poor in this country

We need Health Care in this country
good schools and day care, too
full art funding is a must
to put ourselves in view
to lift our voice
to raise our voice
to give us vision of this land

The song of Canada is a chorus
of all we claim to be
it's urban and it's rural
from sea to sea to sea

hear Canadian industries in this song
Canuck hockey, movies too
it's a corporate song

it's a health care song
it's multi-ethnic
multi-language, too

it's young, it's old
it's Black, it's white
Aboriginal, immigrant too
it's disabled and able-bodied
middle-class, working class
all of you

this song is public housing
and high-end real estate
it's the taste of Pacific salmon
or P.E.I. potatoes on my plate

it's Sydney coal
a Paul Coffey goal
a Karen Kain pas-de-deux
it's far east on the Avalon in Newfoundland
a yearly trek to Stratford
it's being an audience for N.F.B.
or National Ballet

Let's do this song the Canadian way
let's raise our voices in that song
let's be a chorus of who we are
and of who we want to be

In this country.

Stories

TALK THAT TALK

The newspaper image didn't even come close to making it. Blurred across the front page of the City Section, Kari's face looked ordinary. Her hair looked ordinary. Like some process. Like straightened hair. Where were her prized and contentious corn-rows?

Kari slammed the disappointing issue down on her desk, slopping the remnants of cold morning coffee over it. There. For one surreal instant her wet-with-coffee image in newsprint looked real. Had life and colour and dimension, like her. Even the prized corn-rows jumped up and declared themselves to be braided Black hair. Nation hair. Black magic. But after the coffee soaked in, the whole thing was worse. She looked like a black smear on the page, with everyone else's words and headlines bleeding through her face. The beautiful, distinctive braids were gone with the coffee.

Kari wandered one hand idly over her head, finding reassurance in the tight and ordered rows and rows of plaits. Her hand played over and over the patterns of hair woven over and under, each a stand-alone part of the whole. Kari shook her head. She revelled in the movement that action set off. Her braids moving in concert; the black curtain of plaits settling back into the landscape of her head.

Hers was a styled corn-row 'do. From a distance it looked corporate enough. A chic, just below chin-length page-boy, with a curvy side part swirling around the left side of her head, giving her a curved under drape at the bottom of the braids. Kari loved to heft that bottom curve in the palm of her hand. Almost as much as she loved that deep black-plaited curtain of hair that hung down over her right eye, *Vogue*-like. And she could tuck it behind her ear as she and her computer terminal raced the clock to some data-entry deadline.

Make no mistake about it, Kari Taylor loved that hairdo. But not as much as she loved what it did to them at work. Got her looked at. Stared at. Moved away from on the streetcar and the elevator — not so cool; but what else is new? Got her talked about but not talked to. Got racist graffiti scrawled on the washroom mirror. (That was a lot harder to take.) Got her ignored when she tabled her reports at department meetings. Got her passed over for promotion and the wage hike attached to it.

But it also got her to grieve her situation to her union local. Got her to talk that talk, that at first was circular and all tangled up with some kind of Black rage and raggedy and impotent Black misery. But then she met Sula. Sula who was born of some kind of Caribbean woman get-up, stand-up survivalist instinct. Taught her to really talk strong and big and Black.

Because of Sula, and because of that place that snapped inside of Kari that said to her head and to her heart—"You're worth more! Get up and say it! Out loud! Don't take this stuff anymore!" Because of all of that, Kari's hair became overnight political—on her terms. Became a fight. Became: "Your-hair-goes-or-you-do!" from her white and judgmental boss, indignant with misplaced energy spent on intolerance.

It was Sula and her sister-women friends from the Carib-Centre who made her see the fear inside all of that white corporate sabre-rattling. That's all it was, Sula and Afua and the others said.

"They're afraid, woman. They say, 'No corn-row or no you, Kari.' Don't buy that 'corporate image' stuff."

"Talk back, woman. Rattle them braids at 'em. You got Union. And you got us, mouth and all!" Big laugh then, all around. It felt so good.

They all put their black and brown and tan heads together over good, hot West Indian food and lots of talk into many late nights. Talk of money and food and green postcards from home and jobs and men. Always men. All of it mixed in with Sula's "strategy talk" to fight back for Kari's hair.

And it worked. Sula knew it would. They all knew it would when they sat around talking or phoned each other to add to the strategy that they coached Kari in. Keeping her focused on how to "talk that talk" at work and as she presented her case in union sessions.

Kari looked at her watch and dispiritedly condemned the soggy newspaper to the waste-basket. Seven-fifty A.M. The office door swung open on the wave of the first early bird arrivals. Kari was the real early bird this morning. One whole hour and two cups of black coffee early. All that time spent staring at her unfamiliar and blurred face on page one of the City Section. And that headline:

BLACK WOMAN WINS HAIR BATTLE!
"THE CORN-ROWS STAY!" SAYS KARI. "AND SO DO I!"

And now you couldn't even see her braids. Kari sucked her teeth in disgust, a parody of her mother's signal of dismissal and dismay. Kari didn't know if she was ready for this morning to begin, or to happen at all. With all of their fake office talk and superficial attention to her. The battle was over but it sure wasn't over in her nervous stomach.

"Kari! Look at you, kid!"

Here they came, waving page one at her like flags of their own fight and victory. Kari had to suppress a derisive snort at the thought of this out-from-nowhere camaraderie. Everybody loves a winner.

"Way to go, Kari!"

"You look some good. Better than Brian Baloney, anyway." That one got laughs all around, even from Kari.

"Gonna stick this up in the lunch room." They drifted on, waving the offending page, propelled toward morning coffee. This morning, Kari's news provided a convenient and valid delay to the start of everyone's day.

Which one of them had been the author of those lipsticked, racist slurs? Kari flopped her hand at them hoping to wave them away from her, this fickle crew of co-workers; hoping that they were in enough of a fog to accept it as a greeting; but for which Kari really meant: "Thanks. That's enough. Get lost."

She switched on her terminal. Somehow that thin, blue glow curtained her from their prattlings and those flapping, bleary, newspaper images which betrayed her in every issue of the paper. Her workload never looked so inviting. She just wanted to work her day away. The impersonal grunt and hum of her terminal the only dialogue she needed or wanted this day.

The distraction of a body at her side. Up close. Pretending to get personal. Kari eyed Marilyn through the blue glow and her corn-row curtain, eye-balled her with a tense and guarded right eye through those rows. Without looking up.

"Kari?" The voice was too treacle. Too maple syrup. Too Nutrasweet to be true.

"You're in the paper. I guess you're happy."

She was gone. This supervisor woman who spat out her words like wormy apple pits. This woman who ten months ago questioned Kari's hair. Dredged up some raggedy old thing about dress codes that didn't even come close to mentioning anybody's hair, let alone Kari's queen corn-rows. This woman wouldn't get the thanks that Kari felt she owed her. This woman who ignited some long-ago fire buried deep in Kari's heart and soul and made her tongue talk Black and loud and strong and public. About her hair and Nationhood and about the lie that they all walked around in and waved like flags of some fake and transparent equality.

Kari turned back to the blue light and to her keys and data.

The terminal grunted at her, prompted her to stroke, enter, delete, save. Prompted her to think that perhaps it was Marilyn Beed who had scrawled the hate notes in red lipstick on the women's washroom mirror. It looked like her shade. It looked like all of their shades of lipstick. No one had 'fessed up. No one had claimed the black song in their heart that had spilled out into cowardly racist invective in red.

Kari turned back to the juggling act of data entry, subliminating her anger, pushing the thoughts and the faces and the idle, persistent Kari-in-the-newspaper talk that buzzed through the office way down 'till she was hardly aware of it.

And in all of that, she tried to find an acceptable place for her joy.

After all, Marilyn Beed, with her pinched-purse lips had been right about one thing. She had won. No more grief about wearing her corn-rows. Or even wearing her hair in a big fluffy, tangled black cloud, if she wanted to. But there was that nasty newspaper photo, capturing her forever in a blur of ordinary white-looking hair. Kari keyed on and tried to concentrate on the joy. It would be better when she could be with Sula and Afua and the others to laugh and shout and party down the joy of this very real winning one for their own Black and female side of things.

A deep and many-layered sigh came rolling up from some ancient hiding place deep inside of her.

"Well, I'd do more than sigh at the likes of this."

Oh, God. Will they just go on about their own business this morning, please! And leave Kari to her own. Kari kept her eyes on screen, data, keystrokes. Key-strokes.

"Well?" the disembodied voice was staying.

Kari looked up and then got up out of her chair and stood stock still, all open mouth and eyes growing wider and wider as they focussed on the thing in front of her.

There on her desk, looking for all the world like her birthday and big brass band all rolled into one was a brilliant burst of colour—all fruit and flowers that sent up a signal of home—the Caribbean! Bird-of-Paradise and passion flower blooms crowded big, fat mango and papaya, breadfruit and date palm, star apple, sapodilla and pomegranate. Kari could feel her heart beating hard and fast as she imagined that community of sister-women putting their hands and their purses together to say this special thing to her. She could see Sula's hand at work all over this big, warm gesture. That was Sula to the core.

Kari hugged herself hard around the middle. She bent down, diving her nose deep into the tropical smells and colours. She wanted to inhale and bite big bites and to wrap herself up in the colour of it all, all at once. She was laughing and crying big, soundless, fat and happy tears and reaching over and around all of it at once. Got to call Sula and the others. How do you say "Thanks" for such a surprise of love and understanding. And sisterhood.

Before she could finish punching out Sula's number, Kari saw there was more. Something was sticking out of a big manilla envelope beneath the over-burdened basket of goodies.

Kari pulled out this something and dropped the phone. There, in eight by ten black and white was a photo of the biggest, blackest, ear-to-ear smiling face. It was her face, all right. But the hair in the photo said it all. It was all-over corn-rowed to death. Big and little fat and long braids and plaits and twists. They were fighting for space all over her little ten year old head. Fighting for space off the page.

These were righteous braids. The kind that Black mothers and the friends of Black mothers cultivate on the heads of little Black girls, and boys too, if they're lucky, for a while at least.

That Sula. She was behind this. Kari had to marvel and then laugh at the bold, managing hand of this Sula woman. Knowing that Kari was right and only needed the strength of Black women's hearts and minds. Only needed to be set free to talk that talk. To get her tongue around it just right. Just exactly right.

But how did Sula get this photo of the ten year old Kari, all braids and that bold, gap-toothed ten-year-old smile? And to send it today with that brilliant basket of the colours and the tastes and the smells of that other home-place.

The blurred and betraying newspaper photo was already history. Sula and the others helped her in everything. In this, too; finding and seeing Kari for real.

Kari reached for the phone again and began punching out Sula's number. In her mind she felt cool and joyful and in control. But if she had passed her own office door and looked in, as others were doing now, she would have seen a joyful Black woman against a splash of greens and fruits and flowers and colours. She would have seen the woman throw back her head. She would have seen her corn-rows dance and fly.

OPEN WINDOWS

The dream was there again last night, waiting on Felicia's pillow when she went to sleep. Actually, it was there the whole time. When she went to bed. While she was getting ready for bed. Pulling off her sweater, folding her skirt. Pulling her bra off over her head in what she thought of as the feminist way of doing it. Secretly glad always that she had only ever removed her bra that way. Ever and always.

In fact, that dream was probably there as she entered the room. Even as she began to rub her eyes as she sat in front of the blue and flickering t.v., getting ready to get sleepy.

The dream. It was always just like it was the time before. Windows. A series of them. Lined up obliquely like half-opened soldiers. Windows shadowed in night-blue light with sheer curtains billowing seductively, sheer-bellied on some unfelt breeze.

Felicia always woke up because of those windows. She felt exposed; felt naked in front of them. All of the selective and probing eyes she had ever stood before seemed to be behind those windows, half-open like lazy, post-coital eyelids.

A workday that followed on the heels of that dream— any day, any time, was bloated and feeling premenstrual. Never mind what part of her own cycle was working on her. The day after the dream was full and tender. She tiptoed around it. Was careful with it. That day, after a night of open windows, was to be endured and gotten through with a big sigh at the end of it.

What to do with that dream, and with the day after it? Felicia hated not knowing. Hated the dream for how it chased her awake each time. Never allowing her to close the breasting curtains. Never allowing her to peer through the lidded, blue-darkened panes.

How could she know what was on the other side? What was she walking away from always?

Felicia began thinking of it as her fingerprint dream. Began remembering things. Snatches of woman-talk. Those almost forgotten summer kitchen nights; her mama's capable hands pulling through Felicia's uncooperative mane of crinkly mohair hair at two years old, and at ten, and finally, reluctantly at fifteen. Every stroke and pull was tempered by love and woven with the woman-talk that sighed up and out of her mother's bosom to mingle with those of her auntie or an older sister or sometimes the Micmac woman from the train.

The almost forgotten half-stories of women in some stage of birthing. Joy and pain and fear and triumph over their bodies all mixed up with memories of tugs on the head. As joyfully remembered as the ghost of some lover's long-ago caress.

What was Felicia remembering about her dream? Was it her dream? Was it her mama's? An auntie's dream? Whose windows were these? Whose to be opened, then be closed, to be looked through into the seductive blue night on the other side of them?

She wanted to know. She wanted an end to those unknowing and unyielding nights and those tired and tender days, so high-strung with questions. Always questions with no answers.

Felicia planned for the next dream of windows with no answers. She felt her arms reaching and reaching through the window-space, pushing through the blue darkness, moving curtains. Moving back the night.

She was aware of the women in her dreams and in her memories. She could feel the rush of all of those women's sighs, the breath of their worries and their words warm on her neck, her breast growing warm with anticipation.

These are not her windows to open. And these are not her arms to push through the open blue-black puzzle of beckoning night outside of them. These arms are heavy with everyone else's bones and bloodstreams and heavy or taut or hanging blue black brown or nut brown woman skin.

Mama's hands tugging through her stubborn kinks. Sweet Auntie's hands stabbing the air trailing black and broken fingernails; their bits left on some lady's knickers, on some lady's washing in a day's-work house. Somewhere.

The Micmac woman lends Felicia her arms, too, for the dream. These arms are silent and laden with baskets the colour of blue-berries and radishes. All of those arms. Pushing and pushing and interrogating those windows and those night-bellied curtains.

Why only those women's arms in that dream? Why not their heads, or at least their mouths? She needed her mother's or her auntie's mouth to tell her. To speak about windows always half open in the dream. Windows dressed in blowing curtains, full-bellied and breaking the blue-black night beyond them. Windows mocking her with those post-coital lids. Half open, half closed. No one to tell her. No hands to tug at her head and to match the rhythm of windows and woman-talk in her sleep.

THROUGH MY CLASSROOM DOOR

Ici On Parle Egalite

My classroom floor is beachsand beige
the hallway floor is toffee-brown
and sometimes
standing astride the threshold
my right foot on beachsand tile domain
I say
"Ici on parle egalite."

here, inside this box of desks
of chalk and dust and the ghost of countless poems
and lessons
here, we speak equality
no bias of culture race or class
to break the ebb and flow
of word
of thought
of love
of life
so young, so new
and burgeoning in its revolving door of
youth and of discovery

Ici on parle egalite.

we weigh and measure each word
each thought
with a laugh
a tear
with a wish to hold fast
the heart
and to fly skyward
in many tongues and colours
without bounds
no horizon in sight.

How Many Children Do You Have, Miss?

How many children do you have, Miss?
the question earnest and serious
from this fresh and Celtic face
on the Avalon in Newfoundland

my answer
so glib and flip
"...Well...hmmm...160 this year," I say
raising my eyebrow just so
bowing my lips to get the laugh
which comes on cue

the truth hangs like a bubble in the air
the waves of iridescence rainbow its
invisible surface
reflects the annual motherlove
earth-mother extant for all
enroute to the world.

Grad Portrait Gallery

And as I drift by you each day
many times
past the years and years of
two inch by two inch graduates in that high school hall
your decades of eyes
echoes of who you were
rare hints of who you are now
I hear the then and now call your names
down all the days of what was then

so many flights to everywhere

and I
impaled by the calendar of styles of dress
of hair
cannot hurry past
no winged Mercury at my heels
instead I lull and croon
catching the eye of Shelley and of Rob
two songbirds
one Black, the other white
I lull and croon some Neil Young song
as I did with you then
to catch my youth in corners
and to hold
to hold.

High School Confidential

bellies
big and little
swelling under the push of gestation
destination: parenthood

class change
the cola roar of feet
doubletime on hallway stair
up and up to Math
to French
to Computer Class

too many couples
engaged enroute in the exchange of
unwelcome glance
unwelcome touch
of tongue too deep
and of bruises that
shirts and sore young hearts keep

the terminology test
never asks the definition of
teenage angst
and rage
and rage.

Head Count: Black Students In My Academic Nest

the drift
the crowd, and then
the ones and the twos of you
the odd and too few
dark faces in a class set of you
we eye-connect
across a sea of chalkdust
and of desks
Black students in my academic nest
at arms length
I hear and I share your bravado and your banter
I jump-back time
I am you again

we know the beast-beat of salmon
against the tide
against the tide

Too Few Of You

And you
young pride of Lake Loon
of Preston
and of Cherrybrook
you
so hurry-footed to the edge of life
headstrong
headful of the academic banter
the currency of English Lit/Math credits
exchanged
traded up for a place in the sun

I hear the prideful whisper and applause
of the old guard all around you
they cheer you from the rim of hope
and of time gone by
Marie Hamilton
Ruth Johnson
W.P. Oliver
Pearleen Oliver
Wilhemina Williams
Edith Clayton
Daureen Lewis
Rose Fortune
Portia White
Portia White

they reach for you
call your name from
the roll of pioneers

"Swing wide the door to
success," they say
"To life!
To life!

Climb that ladder!
Seize that day!
your moment to
break ground
break free."

too few of you
stand with that glad and
shallow-breathing crowd
on the day of graduates
my heart connects and
tattoos out my pride
my hope
my joy for you

I catch my self mid-joy
seeing only the ones
the tens
too few of you

too many stumble
fall
don't heed the call from the margins
then fall from hope
from the centre
then
that terrible echo of metal on flesh
coffles of old strike fear into
this new face and
heart of darkness.

Class Change: Young Lions On The Tide

And standing at my classroom door
to see the sea and flood of you
waves of young bodies
adrift from French to Gym to Computers to me
exploring Literature from ode to ode
I see the wave and flood of you
turning corners
leaving youth in your wake

and from the belly of the wave
as you change courses
change classes
you emerge, Black youth
young lions male and female
of far and distant Africa
trading beads and denim
big ticket leathers and runners
up-market flags of this new age

and as you crest the wave
turning corners
coming to, then
passing by my classroom door
I see your wounds
young lions
young pride of old Africa
eyes reflecting elusive dreams
quick fun
quick cash
too many dreams of the genie in the slam dunk
and parenthood too soon
                too soon
mark you
caught and held
in the jaws of this new bondage.

BLACK STAR RISING

Black Star Rising

With thanks to Alice Walker for finding Zora Neale Hurston again.

How to thank you, Alice Walker
for finding that trail to Zora
gone cold
with pedantic and other eyes elsewhere
on literary giants Black and white
male/female
old and new

how did you find that trail
to Eatonville Florida, Alice?

your feet, dragging and dancing
in those earth and heavenly ruts
made by mules
your eyes also watching God.

And did your heart beat and beat
fast and faster
as you walked the path of Janie
and of Tea Cake?

And did the path grow hot beneath you
hot and hotter still
as you found
and asked
and read and read
and hand over hand over heart over mind
found your way to Eatonville,
found your way back to Zora?

Zora In My Heart

In praise of African-American literary woman-pioneer Zora Neale Hurston (1891-1960)

    Carrying Zora in my heart
    makes me bigger than I am
    my poet's soul
    a monument
    to her
    that woman-hero
    pioneer spirit in flight

The Dream Of Dogs And Presidents

The dream of dogs and presidents
arrests me in the sweep of the day
half in wakefulness
half in dreamstate
the little dog
all tongue and ears
and happy wagging tail
does that puppy half-trot stumble
through the air
so up close tough familiar
and so real
I reach for the glitter
of that wet and happy nose
and then
and then
the dog evaporates, tongue first
flopping ears and tail fades last
to leave, in his cuddle-brown wake
this big-haired man named Bill
and me
to stand together
behind some presidential shield
in some big plush and spit-shined
New York hotel with *plaza* in its name
with red carpet on the floor
just big-haired Bill and me
we stand
we smile
we press the flesh
I in purple and red
he in old boys' navy
it sets off the grey
that big and boyish head a wag
all grins
all toothsome airbrushed smile

I wonder
does he mistake me for that
mother confessor to the world
with a name that starts with "O"?
or, much happier the thought,
he likens Maxine to Maya
with inaugural tome in her future
now in her pop culture past

I see that big grey head named Bill

I surge to a rude awakening
to pluck feathers and sleepdust
from these eyes
so fresh from dreams
of dogs and presidents.